Published by Curious Fox, an imprint of Capstone Global Library
Limited, 264 Banbury Road, Oxford, OX2 7DY – Registered company
number: 6695582

www.curious-fox.com

ISBN 978-1-78202-499-6
20 19 18 17 16
10 9 8 7 6 5 4 3 2

A CIP catalogue for this book is available from the British Library.

Printed and bound in China.

The Sleuths of Somerville

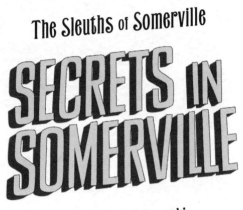

SECRETS IN SOMERVILLE

by Michele Jakubowski

Curious Fox
a capstone company-publishers for children

CHAPTER ONE

Somerville isn't a place you go to visit – it's the small town you go through on the way to the place you're heading to. Watertown, a bigger town about 50 kilometres down the main road from Somerville, is a place to visit. Travellers stop in Somerville, though, for two things Watertown doesn't have: cheap petrol and the delicious doughnuts at Mick's Diner.

Amelia and Jason Vega, the proud owners of Mick's Diner, adored living in Somerville. Between the tourists stopping for food and a town full of regular customers, their restaurant stayed busy. Their children, twelve-year-old Rowan and eleven-year-old Astrid, on the other hand, weren't so excited about living in sleepy little Somerville.

School had just broken up for the summer, and instead of doing anything fun, Rowan and Astrid were sitting at the counter of their parents' restaurant, rolling silverware into napkins. "Why can't we move to Watertown?" Rowan asked for what felt like the millionth time.

"Yeah," said Astrid. "They've got a water park and a zoo. They even have a shopping centre. Somerville is so boring!"

"In my day we didn't have the luxury of getting bored," came a voice from the end of the counter.

Rowan and Astrid turned to face the owner of that voice, Mrs Coretta Lownie, or Miss Coco, as all the townspeople called her. Miss Coco was the oldest living resident of Somerville and a regular at the restaurant. She spent whole days sitting at the counter at Mick's telling stories to anyone who would listen. Sometimes those stories even made sense.

"Oh no, Miss Coco?" Rowan replied.

"Heavens, no!" Miss Coco began. "We were up before dawn, feeding the chickens and the pigs. Then we nearly broke our backs tending to the garden. But if those chores weren't done, there'd be no food for any of us!"

Rowan and Astrid lowered their heads, feeling guilty about their complaining.

Miss Coco went on, "Then we walked twelve miles to school each day. Uphill both ways. With no shoes *and* in the snow. Speaking of snow, I remember the year it snowed marshmallows. Big, fluffy ones, not those little puny ones you find in your hot chocolate. We collected them up in baskets to roast over the fire . . ."

Rowan lifted his head. "Wait, what?"

"Let it go, sweetie," Mrs Vega whispered.

"You're right, Miss Coco," Mr Vega said, winking at his children. "These spoiled kids don't know the meaning of hard work and helping others."

"If you're bored, come over to the garage," said another customer, Marcus Sloane. Marcus had been running Earl's Petrol Station across the street from the restaurant ever since the owner, Earl Bigby, had retired and moved to Florida. He may not have been the most qualified for the job, but he certainly was enthusiastic about it.

"We've got so many cool tools over there!" Marcus continued. "I don't even know what half of them do. There's one that looks like it could slice a car in two!"

As Rowan and Astrid's eyes grew wider, Mrs Vega interrupted the excited Marcus. "That's okay, Marcus! I think we can find plenty of things for the kids to do here."

Rowan groaned. "But that's just it. There's nothing to do!"

"There is plenty to do in Somerville," his mum replied firmly.

"But everything there is to do in Somerville we've already done – many times!" Astrid argued.

"She's right," Rowan said, a statement he rarely uttered about his younger sister. "Somerville is too small. We know every person who lives here! There are never any new people, and we know all there is to know about the people who already live here."

"I sincerely doubt that," Miss Coco said as she took a sip of her coffee.

Mr Vega placed his hands on the counter and leaned towards Rowan and Astrid. In a hushed voice he asked, "You kids want excitement and adventure?"

"Yes!" they said.

"Then make it!" he exclaimed. "Shake things up every once in a while! Adventure is all around you every single day."

Astrid and Rowan rolled their eyes and groaned yet again. Astrid playfully threw a balled-up napkin at her dad.

"What's that supposed to mean?" Rowan asked.

"It doesn't even make sense!" Astrid said.

"Who knows?" Mr Vega said. He pointed towards the restaurant's front door. "Maybe excitement and adventure are right on the other side of that door at this very moment."

Astrid threw another napkin at her dad. Then the bell on the restaurant's door chimed. In walked a very pretty young woman with dark hair and a tall boy about Rowan's age. Both were carrying suitcases and looked startled when everyone in Mick's Diner stopped what they were doing.

The clock on the wall ticked three times before anyone spoke.

Mrs Vega finally broke the silence and said, "Welcome to Somerville!"

CHAPTER TWO

"So, what happened next?" asked Astrid's best friend, Quinn. She sat on the edge of the bed, listening raptly as Astrid told her about the two strangers who had walked into Mick's Diner.

"I was totally freaked out at first!" Astrid said. She paced and gestured wildly as she told the story. She loved an audience, especially when she had a good tale to tell. "I thought maybe they were aliens or something! I mean, the way they just appeared like that after my dad said that thing about adventure on the other side of the door. It was all so crazy!"

Astrid also tended to be a bit dramatic. Luckily, Quinn was used to it.

She went on, "What are the chances? It was like they were just waiting outside for us to say something like that so they could barge in and, I don't know, attack us or something!"

Perhaps Astrid was more than a bit dramatic. Quinn knew this and waited impatiently for her friend to finish the story.

"But obviously they weren't aliens and they didn't attack anyone," she said, prompting Astrid along. "So, who were they?"

"The boy's name is Jace, and he's twelve like Rowan. He looks older, though, because he's really tall. Or maybe he's normal height – it's hard to tell because Rowan is such a shrimp!"

Even though Rowan was fourteen months older than Astrid – a fact he never let her forget – the two were the same height. Their mum reassured Rowan that he would eventually have a growth spurt and be tall like his dad, but Astrid still loved to tease him.

"Who was the pretty girl with him?" Quinn asked.

"Turns out she's his mum," Astrid said. "She must be one of those people who look really young for their age. Her name is Evie, and she seems really nice. She asked us to call her by her first name. You'll get to know her. She's going to be working at the restaurant."

"What?" Quinn's eyes widened. She slapped her hands on the bed, almost causing her to fall to the floor. "Did your parents know they were coming? Is that how your dad did the whole 'adventure-on-the-other-side-of-the-door' thing?"

"No, that's one of the weird things," Astrid said. "They just moved here out of the blue. Evie didn't even have a job lined up."

"That *is* weird," Quinn agreed.

"My mum just started talking to her, and you know how my mum can be." Astrid motioned with her hand as if she were making a puppet talk. "She can talk to anyone, and five minutes later she's got his or her life story. As soon as she found out Evie didn't have a job, she offered her one. They'd been looking for help, anyway, so it all worked out."

"Wow," Quinn said. Quinn's family had lived in town for four generations. Her father was the town doctor, just like her grandfather, great-grandfather and great-great-grandfather had been. That's the way it was with most families in Somerville.

Quinn was letting the surprise arrival of new residents in Somerville sink in when she remembered something Astrid had said.

"So, what's the other weird thing?" she asked.

"Huh?" Astrid asked. She had just sat down, exhausted after telling her story.

Quinn reminded her, "You said, 'One of the weird things' when you told me Evie came to town without a job."

"Oh, yeah." Astrid jumped to her feet and began pacing again. "I almost forgot the craziest part! Guess where they're living."

Quinn prided herself on being able to figure things out quickly. She thought for a moment. "The B&B?"

The B&B was the bed and breakfast across the street from Mick's Diner run by Mrs Joanne Cheever. She'd inherited the giant old house from her family. After her kids moved away and her husband died, she turned it into a source of lodging for people looking for a place to stay that was off the main road. Much to the benefit of the Vega family, guests usually did the breakfast part at the restaurant – Mrs Cheever was a notoriously awful cook.

Astrid rolled her eyes. "What would be weird about that? No, no, no! Think weirder. I'm talking off-the-charts weird."

The whole story had been off-the-charts weird to Quinn. She was trying to wrap her mind around the facts that there were new people living in Somerville and that the restaurant had a new employee. She tried to think of the strangest place the newcomers could be living. It took Quinn another moment, but finally her brain sorted it out.

"The Potters' place?" said Quinn

Astrid nodded.

"No way," said Quinn.

"Way," said Astrid.

CHAPTER THREE

The Potters' place was a big, old house that sat up on a hill a few blocks off Main Street. There were as many rumours about the place as there were residents of Somerville, but the prevailing story went back to the founding of the town. The Potter family was one of the original groups who made the trek out West and established Somerville. Some say the original founders were lazy, and when they saw the mountains off in the distance they said, "This looks like a nice spot" – and never left.

The story goes that the Potters were not well liked and had joined the group uninvited. They built their house away from the others and kept to themselves. Even with the distance, though, whenever anything bad happened to the townspeople, it was always blamed on the Potters. Accidents, illnesses, sudden deaths or even bad weather could be traced back to some member of the Potter family. As you can imagine, all this blame made them very paranoid people, and it eventually drove them crazy.

One night a fire broke out at the Potters' place. After debate and delay, the townspeople went to help, and the fire was quickly put out. When some townspeople went inside, they couldn't find any members of the Potter family. All of their belongings, right down to their shoes and money, remained, but there was no sign of the family. Nobody would miss them, but how and why had they gone without taking anything? Had they just disappeared?

Stories grew in the days, months and years to follow. Many people in Somerville thought the house was haunted or, at a minimum, cursed, and wouldn't go near it. It had been abandoned for as long as any living resident of the town could remember.

"I hear that when the wind blows from that direction at night, you can hear the family crying for help in the attic," Astrid said.

Astrid, Quinn and Rowan were all at Mick's Diner helping clean up after the breakfast rush.

"Has anyone even been in that house in the last hundred years?" Quinn asked. "It's got to be full of spiders and bats!"

Rowan, who was clearing dishes off a nearby table, shrugged and said, "I don't know. I think it'd be pretty cool to live there."

"What?" Astrid stopped wiping the counter one final time and looked incredulously at her brother. "You're afraid to even walk near the Potters' place. When we wanted to go out there last Halloween, you said no way."

Rowan turned back to the table he was clearing and mumbled, "It was cold that night, and I thought I was coming down with something."

"Don't you find it odd that the new people *want* to live there?" Quinn asked.

"No odder than them moving to Somerville in the first place," Astrid replied.

"People move all the time," Rowan piped in. He had hung out a little with Jace the day before, while their mums discussed the job at the restaurant. While Rowan had plenty of friends in Somerville, he wasn't particularly social and didn't have any close friendships like Astrid and Quinn's. He had been immediately comfortable with Jace and was now feeling defensive for his new friend. "Why shouldn't they move to Somerville?"

Astrid retorted, "Why would anyone *want* to move to Somerville?"

"Hey!" Mr Vega said. "Your mum and I moved to Somerville, and we love it here. Besides, those rumours about the Potters' place are just old wives' tales."

"Oh, yeah?" asked Astrid. "Would you spend the night at the Potters' place?"

Mr Vega stopped stocking the doughnut case and stammered, "Well, uh . . ."

Much to his relief, the restaurant's door chimed and in walked Evie and Jace.

"Well, look who's here," Mr Vega called jovially. While he was happy to see them, he was also glad to not have to answer his daughter's question.

Mrs Vega had heard the door and came out from the kitchen. "Well, hello, Evie. Hello, Jace," she said.

"Hello, Mrs Vega," Evie said.

"Oh, please, honey, call me Amelia," Mrs Vega said and put her arm around Evie's shoulder. In the same way her son had hit it off right away with Jace, Mrs Vega had felt an almost motherly affection towards her new employee. "Welcome to Mick's Diner. Come on in the office. I've got some paperwork for you to fill out." She guided Evie to the back office and called over her shoulder, "Jace, help yourself to a doughnut. They're still warm."

Jace, who was tall and lanky, lumbered slowly over to the counter, hiding his face behind his fringe.

"Jace, you remember our kids, Rowan and Astrid. This is Quinn, Astrid's best friend," Mr Vega said, putting a doughnut on a plate in front of Jace.

"So," Astrid said, "how was sleeping at the Potters' place? Did anything scary happen?"

"Astrid!" Mr Vega scolded her, while leaning closer to Jace to hear his answer.

"Don't listen to them," Rowan said quickly, taking a seat at the counter next to Jace. "They don't know what they're talking about."

Jace looked confused but let out a small laugh. He took a bite of his doughnut. "This is amazing," he said.

"Best doughnuts in town," Mr Vega said proudly. "Tell us about yourself, Jace. I don't know if you said the other day where you two are from."

Jace shifted a little in his chair and waved his hand vaguely. "Oh, you know, out East."

"The East Coast?" Mr Vega asked. "My wife and I are from New York. Are you from that area?"

"Um, well," Jace rambled. He rubbed the back of his neck and looked down as he mumbled, "Sort of, you know, the, um, New York area in general . . ."

Rowan noticed that Jace's face had grown a bright shade of red and decided to rescue him. "Do you like video games?" he asked.

"Yes!" Jace practically shouted. It was the most animated he'd been since walking into the restaurant.

"Do you play *Gideon's Grave*?" Rowan asked.

"I love that game!" Jace said.

Soon the two were caught up in a conversation about strategies and game play. Before long the restaurant began to fill up with the lunch crowd, and Jace joined Astrid, Rowan and Quinn in helping out. By the time the last customers were served, Jace had become like one of the gang, joking comfortably and laughing. Jace's humour and good-naturedness quickly won over Quinn and Astrid the same way it had Rowan. The fun times ended suddenly, though, when Mrs Ruth Partridge barged through the door.

"Help!" she shouted. "Rex is missing!"

CHAPTER FOUR

"Who's Rex?" Jace asked Rowan.

"Her dog," Rowan whispered back.

"My Rex! My Rex!" Mrs Partridge wailed.

Ruth Partridge was 75 years old and the curator of the town's museum. Her beloved pooch, Rex, was a Jack Russell terrier that never left her side. For years Mrs Partridge had raised dogs that were treated better than some of the children in town.

"It's okay, Mrs Partridge," Mrs Vega said, patting the elderly woman on the shoulder. "I'm sure Rex will come home soon."

"It's that Doherty girl!" Mrs Partridge shouted. "I just know it. She's had it in for Rex ever since she came back to town! She should close down that shop and get out of town."

"Now, Mrs Partridge," Mr Vega said in a calm voice. "Why would Delilah want to harm Rex?"

Mrs Partridge huffed and ignored the question.

Delilah Doherty owned a sweet shop called the Sugar Shack next door to the museum. Originally from Somerville, Delilah had moved to Paris after high school to study baking and sweet-making. Her return to Somerville after her studies had been celebrated by the townspeople – except for Mrs Partridge, for some strange reason. No one understood her dislike of Delilah.

"We'll help you find Rex," Rowan spoke up.

For the first time since she'd rushed in, the colour returned to Mrs Partridge's face. "You will?"

"Yes," Rowan replied and turned toward Jace. "We all will."

Jace smiled and nodded, happy to be included. "Don't worry. We'll find your dog."

Jace, Rowan, Quinn and Astrid headed down Main Street, away from Highway 84 and towards the town square, calling for Rex as they walked. Rowan and Jace walked on one side of the street, while Astrid and Quinn were on the other side.

"So, are you into sports?" Rowan asked. He liked to watch sports and had a good mind for stats, but he wasn't much of an athlete.

"Sure," Jace responded. "My favourites are baseball, football, cycling –"

"Cycling?" Rowan interrupted. "You mean like bike races?"

"They're awesome!" Jace's eyes lit up. "Cycling is really big in Europe. They do these crazy climbs in the mountains! One time, my dad and I . . ."

Jace stopped walking and went quiet for a second. When he started talking again, his excitement had cooled. "Well, one time I went to a race. It was great. You should check it out."

"I will," Rowan responded. "Sounds fun."

After a moment of awkward silence, Rowan said, "So, it must have been hard leaving your friends when you moved."

Jace shrugged. "Not really. We move a lot, so I never really get the chance to make good friends."

"Do you like moving around?" Rowan asked. He, like most people in town, had lived in Somerville his whole life.

Jace looked down, sending his dark hair over his eyes. "You get used to it. We lived in the last place for less than six months. I didn't even bother getting to know anyone."

"I don't know what's worse," Rowan said with a chuckle. "Moving a lot or being stuck in the same place your whole life!"

Jace looked up and smiled. "I think it would be nice to live in one place for a long time. I bet you've got a lot of good friends."

Rowan thought about it for a moment. While he knew all of the kids his own age in town, and got along well with them, he didn't really feel like he could consider many of them "good friends". He certainly had never had a best friend the way Astrid did with Quinn.

"The kids are nice here," he said finally.

"Tell me about Somerville," Jace said. "Seems like a pretty odd place."

Rowan laughed. "It's not interesting enough to be odd! Somerville is a typical small town with not much to do." Rowan thought of the conversation in the restaurant earlier, questioning why anyone would want to move to Somerville. He hesitated briefly before saying, "Actually, I was sort of surprised that you and your mum moved here."

"You and me both," Jace said with a laugh and a shake of his head.

Rowan could tell that Jace didn't like talking about himself, but before he could stop himself, he blurted out, "So why did you?"

Jace shoved his hands in his pockets and turned away, making Rowan sorry he had asked. Before Jace could reply, Rowan added, "It's none of my business. Never mind."

"No, it's okay," Jace said, turning back to face Rowan. He took a deep breath before speaking again. "We . . ."

"There is no sign of Rex anywhere!" Astrid called as she ran across the street towards the boys. "Not a hair or a pawprint to be found."

"We've looked everywhere there is to look," Quinn said with frustration.

Rowan and Jace were quiet. Rowan didn't know what Jace was about to say, but he felt like it was important. It made him happy to think that Jace had felt comfortable enough to share whatever it was with him.

"Hello?" Astrid said waving her hand in front of her brother's face. "Earth to Rowan! Wake up! What is wrong with you two? Were you guys even looking for Rex?"

"Of course we were!" Rowan said, annoyed with his sister. "There's no sign of him anywhere. Something is definitely going on here."

"What do we do now?" Quinn asked.

A serious look crossed Rowan's face. "Start interviewing suspects," he replied.

CHAPTER FIVE

It may be comical to refer to a sweet-maker as "sweet", but that was the perfect word to describe Delilah Doherty. The youngest of the six Doherty daughters, Delilah was the only one who had left Somerville for an extended amount of time. She was also the only unmarried sister. The other Doherty girls had all gone to college in Watertown before settling down in

Somerville. When Delilah announced she wanted to study sweet-making in Paris, her family was shocked.

Delilah had always been creative. She loved to make things and from a young age was an amazing baker. With the help of the school's guidance counsellor, Delilah quietly researched schools around the world and applied to the best ones. It wasn't until she had been accepted to a school in Paris that Delilah told her family her plans.

At first they tried to change her mind. How could a meek, young girl like Delilah live overseas by herself? But Delilah dug in her heels, and eventually her parents gave in.

Delilah thrived in Paris. She loved the culture and delicious food. She graduated at the top of her class and had offers to work in New York, London and San Francisco. Delilah missed Somerville, though, and it had always been her plan to move home and open a sweet shop. The Sugar Shack did very well, and even with Somerville's poor Internet service, Delilah had a booming online business. With the exception of having her parents pester her to find a husband, Delilah loved her life in Somerville and was well liked. Was there any reason to believe she would steal Mrs Partridge's dog?

As Rowan, Astrid, Jace and Quinn walked into the Sugar Shack, they were distracted from their mission by the overwhelmingly delicious smells of sugar and chocolate. The front of the shop was small and featured an L-shaped glass counter on two sides of the room, at the end of which sat an old-fashioned cash till. Behind the glass of the counter was every kind of delectable treat imaginable. There were truffles, chocolate creams in all flavours, fudge, nut clusters, toffee, brittle, caramels. You name it, Delilah made it, all fresh and handmade. On the other side of the room were shelves upon shelves stacked with glass jars filled with every flavour of jelly bean, boiled sweets, chews, lollipops and licorice.

When she heard the front door open, Delilah came out from the kitchen in the back, carrying a shiny silver tray.

"Well, hello, guys!" Delilah greeted her visitors with a bright smile. "You are just in time. I'm setting out a fresh batch of caramels. Try one and tell me what you think."

Delilah was a petite young woman who kept her red hair in a sleek, chin-length bob. She was wearing jeans and a bright-white T-shirt, with an orange apron bearing the name of her shop.

"Hard to believe this lady could have stolen anyone's dog," Jace whispered to Rowan.

"I agree," Rowan whispered back. "But you never know around here."

They popped caramels into their mouths and chewed. And chewed. And chewed some more.

"These are delicious!" Astrid said with a mouth full of gooey caramel.

"Close your mouth when you're chewing," said Rowan. "That's disgusting."

"Sorry," Astrid mumbled sheepishly and swallowed.

"I'm just glad you like them," Delilah chuckled. She motioned towards Jace. "Who's your friend?"

"Oh, sorry," Rowan said, embarrassed to now be the rude one. "This is Jace. He and his mum just moved here."

"Is that right?" Delilah smiled. "It's so nice to meet you! Where are you from?"

Jace looked down, shaking his dark hair over his eyes. His cheeks reddened as he gave his standard vague reply, "Out East . . ."

Rowan thought of what Jace had said about moving around a lot. He figured that Jace was tired of explaining it and wanted to spare him the discomfort. "It's a small town," he said. "Even my parents had never heard of it."

The lie caught Astrid's attention. "What? When did they hear –"

Rowan cut off his sister by stuffing another caramel in her mouth. "Have another, Astrid, since you love them so much."

Astrid was confused, but she didn't want to be accused of talking with her mouth full of sweets again. Jace and Rowan smiled at each other with relief.

Rowan gave a small thumbs-up to his friend before turning back to Delilah.

"Not only did we want to show Jace your awesome shop, we also wanted to ask you if you've seen Rex today," he said.

Delilah's smile immediately vanished. "You mean Mrs Partridge's snippy little dog?" she said, scowling.

All four of them were surprised by Delilah's change in tone. Never before had they seen Delilah so openly annoyed. And annoyed with a harmless little dog like Rex?

"Um, yeah," Quinn answered. "We're helping Mrs Partridge look for him."

Delilah smiled a tight smile and said, "I haven't seen him today."

Astrid swallowed her caramel and said, "He's been missing all day, and Mrs Partridge is very worried. We said we would help her find him."

"Well, he's not here," Delilah said as she turned and walked behind the counter. Her abrupt change in mood confused them all.

Rowan proceeded cautiously. "And you haven't seen him lately?" he asked. "You know how much he means to Mrs Partridge."

"Look," Delilah said sharply, "I don't mean to seem cold, but it's just that Mrs Partridge has not been the best neighbour since I opened the shop. She obviously doesn't like me, no matter how hard I've tried. Honestly, I'm at my wit's end with this strange feud she's started between us!"

Rowan, Jace, Astrid and Quinn stood still and exchanged glances, not sure what to do next.

Delilah took a deep breath and seemed to relax a little bit. In a softened tone, she said, "Why don't you try the dog park? Seems like a logical place for a runaway dog to go. Or maybe hang some signs? I'll let you know right away if Rex turns up here."

They all thanked Delilah for the sweets before heading out of the store.

"Well, that was really weird," Quinn said, frowning and crossing her arms. "I knew that Mrs Partridge didn't like Delilah, but did you notice that Delilah called whatever it was going on between them a 'feud'? That seems pretty extreme."

"Yes," Rowan replied. "She also said she was at her wit's end. Could she be mad enough to have taken Rex?"

CHAPTER SIX

The sugar buzz they received from Delilah's caramels quickly faded as the foursome stood on the pavement in front of the Sugar Shack.

"Now what?" asked Quinn.

"I don't know," Rowan replied. "While I think Delilah is definitely frustrated with Mrs Partridge, I still don't know if she took Rex."

"I just don't get it," Quinn said, shaking her head. "That dog is treated like a king. I heard Mrs Partridge even buys him steak at Goodwin's Market."

"I heard that, too," Astrid said. "And when she eats at the restaurant, she doesn't just get Rex a doggie bag – he gets his own meal, on a plate and everything."

The four stood in silence for a moment, not sure of what to do next.

"We're right here," Astrid said. "Maybe we should check in with Mrs Partridge to see if Rex has come home yet."

The Somerville Museum was located next door to the Sugar Shack on Main Street. Mrs Partridge lived in a flat above the museum. At the top of the stairs, they found the front door wide open.

"Hello?" Rowan called as the four of them stepped into the flat. They were startled to find a woozy-looking Mrs Partridge in the front room. The curtains were drawn, and the room felt as depressing as the sad, faded couch on which she was lying.

"Rex? Is that you?" she said as she sat up halfway,

the old couch creaking beneath her, with that small movement seeming to take a lot of effort.

"Don't get up, Mrs Partridge. It's just us," Astrid said as she crossed the room. It was so dark in there that she tripped on Mrs Partridge's shoes, which had been left in the middle of the floor, and banged her knee on the solid wood coffee table.

"Oh!" Mrs Partridge said as she halfheartedly tried again to sit up. "Have you found my Rex?"

"Don't worry about me," Astrid grumbled beneath her breath, rubbing her sore knee. "I'm fine."

Quinn answered Mrs Partridge. "No, not yet."

The old woman looked so pathetic lying in the cave-like darkness.

"Are you okay, Mrs Partridge?" Rowan asked. "Can we get you anything?"

Mrs Partridge lay back down, placing her arm over her eyes. "I'm all right. I just need my Rex."

Quinn asked, "Mrs Partridge, was my dad here?"

Mrs Partridge removed her arm and squinted her eyes. Instead of looking at Quinn, however, she looked in Jace's direction. "Who are you?" she asked. "I don't even know you. Why would your dad be here? Did you take my dog?"

Jace looked frightened. "I, uh . . ."

Stepping in front of Jace, Quinn said, "No, Mrs Partridge, me, Quinn Ramsey. My dad is Dr Ramsey. Did he stop by to see you?"

Mrs Partridge blinked a few times before responding. "Yes, he was just here. He fixed me a nice cup of chamomile tea and said I should get some rest."

The room was quiet, and for a moment the kids thought Mrs Partridge had fallen asleep. Rowan motioned towards the door, and they began to tiptoe out. Suddenly Mrs Partridge broke the silence and exclaimed, "The Larsens' dog!"

Jace, Quinn and Rowan all stopped in their tracks. Astrid, on the other hand, dropped to the floor.

"What are you doing?" Rowan whispered in annoyance, helping his sister back up.

"I panicked," Astrid explained, embarrassed.

"So you fell to the floor?" Rowan hissed.

Quinn stepped towards the couch. "What's that, Mrs Partridge?"

"The Larsens' dog! That mangy old mutt. He's a ferocious beast. I don't like the way he looks at my precious Rex," Mrs Partridge said, her arm still over her eyes.

"Is she even awake?" Astrid whispered.

Quinn shrugged and whispered back, "I don't even think the Larsens have a dog."

The four stood silent as Mrs Partridge mumbled on and on about the Larsens' dog.

"What do you think?" Astrid said finally.

Jace pointed out, "What other leads do we have?"

Rowan sighed deeply. "I guess we're heading to the Larsens'."

CHAPTER SEVEN

The Larsens lived on Lincoln Street, a few blocks east of Main Street. As the foursome walked, they discussed what they would do when they got to the house.

"Do we just barge in and say, 'Do you have a dog? And if so, is it mean? And did you have anything to do with Rex's disappearance? And if you did, why would you steal a little old lady's dog? That's so mean,'" Astrid said in a rush.

"Calm down," Rowan told his sister with a roll of his eyes. "We're not going to storm in and start rambling like crazy people. First of all, let's figure out everything we might know about the Larsens. Who's got something?"

"I, obviously, know them the best," Jace said sarcastically, making the rest of the group chuckle.

"I know that they have a big family," Quinn said. "Five kids, I think, or maybe six."

"Aren't most of them older, though?" Rowan asked. He knew there weren't any Larsen kids in his year or his sister's.

Quinn nodded her head. "That sounds right. I think a few of them may even be married and living on their own."

"I think they have a son in high school," Astrid added. "He was at the restaurant the other night."

Astrid would never admit it out loud, but she was a bit nosy and paid close attention when the high school kids came into the restaurant. To her, they seemed so mature and interesting.

They arrived at the Larsens' house and stood out front on the pavement.

"Okay, so we know they have five or six kids, some of whom may not live here, including one who is in high school and ate at the restaurant recently," Rowan said glumly when he realised what little information they had about the Larsens. He shook his head. "Maybe I don't know everything about everybody in Somerville."

"Maybe we should look around a little and see if Rex is here," Jace suggested.

"Good idea," Astrid said. "You guys check it out, and Quinn and I will stand guard."

Jace and Rowan gave each other a look that made it clear neither of them was thrilled with that plan.

"Um, er," Jace stammered. "I don't really know my way around and, uh . . ."

Rowan helped him out. "Plus, Jace is new in town. People might freak out if they see a stranger lurking around. You two go ahead. We'll keep watch."

"Oh, you big babies," Astrid said in exasperation.

"Let's go, Quinn. First, we'll look in the back garden, and then we'll see if we can peek in the windows."

"If we see someone coming, we'll yell, 'Ca-caw, ca-caw,' like a crow," Rowan said.

Astrid gave him a bewildered look and asked, "Why would you do that?"

Quinn helped her out, saying, "So we'll know someone is coming and can get out of here. If that happens, let's meet up back at the restaurant."

"Oh!" Astrid smiled. "Cool plan. I like it. It's very secret agent-ish."

They didn't get to use their cool plan, though, because as Astrid and Quinn began to walk away, a beat-up old car pulled up in front of the house. A teenage boy got out and walked towards them. He was dressed in white trousers and a white short-sleeved, button-up shirt. He also wore a black apron and black shoes, both of which had splashes of what appeared to be blood on them.

"Ca-caw! Ca-caw!" Astrid shouted and spun in a circle.

"Stop it!" Rowan hissed as he grabbed her arm. "Act cool!"

"Is she okay?" the boy asked as he walked towards them. As he got closer, he pointed to Astrid. "Hey! I know you. You're the girl who spilled water on me at Mick's Diner."

Astrid blushed as the rest of the group laughed. Astrid had, indeed, spilled water on the boy when he was at the restaurant with a group of friends. She had been trying to eavesdrop on their conversation and didn't realise the glass she was refilling had started running over.

"Yeah, sorry about that," Astrid mumbled, looking anywhere but at the boy.

"No worries," he smiled. "Can I help you guys?"

"Do you live here?" Quinn asked, pointing to the Larsens' house.

"I sure do," he replied. "I'm Anthony Larsen. What can I do for you?"

"Is that . . . ?" Jace started, pointing at Anthony's shoes. All of the colour drained from his face and his knees bent slightly. He looked as if he were on the verge of fainting. Quinn was standing next to him and quickly grabbed his arm to steady him. Her eyes went from Jace to where he had been pointing, and she immediately turned the same shade of pale. Rowan and Astrid stepped in to steady the pair before one of them took a nasty fall.

"Blood?" Anthony asked with a smirk. He seemed amused at Quinn's and Jace's aversion to blood. "It is. I work at Goodwin's Market. I just got promoted to the meat department. It's awesome."

Quinn kept her eyes up. She couldn't even look at Anthony. "How is that awesome?" she wanted to know.

Anthony told her, "It's awesome because I got a big raise and a whole load of new responsibilities. Plus, I make so much money now I'm going to take my girlfriend, Kayla, to Murphy's Steak House in Watertown."

It was hard to know what Anthony was prouder of: his promotion or his girlfriend.

Astrid found the whole scene hilarious and took the opportunity to tease her best friend. "Some doctor you'll make. Afraid of a few drops of blood."

Jace was also avoiding looking directly at Anthony, so Rowan brought things back to the investigation. "We were just helping Mrs Partridge find her dog, Rex. Have you seen him?"

Anthony thought for a moment. "Do you mean that little dog she carries around? I saw them a few weeks ago when I started in the meat department. My boss says she brings him in all the time to get bones and meat scraps. The little guy goes nuts for them."

"And that was the last time you saw him? You're sure?" Rowan asked.

"Yep, it's been a while. I'm not sure why they haven't been in lately. Sorry if that doesn't help," Anthony replied as he started walking towards the house. When the foursome didn't leave, he turned around and added, "I'd like to help you look, but I'm heading back to work. I just came home to get a change of clothes. They're letting me close down the meat department by myself tonight, and I'm taking Kayla to the cinema right afterwards."

He wiggled his shoes towards Quinn and Jace, adding, "Wouldn't want to wear bloodstained shoes to the cinema."

Anthony chuckled as Jace's and Quinn's faces went from a ghostly white to a greenish colour.

"Wait!" Rowan called after him. Anthony stopped and turned around. "Do you have a dog?"

"Yeah." Anthony looked confused. "Why?"

Rowan kept thinking about what Mrs Partridge had said about the Larsens' dog. He believed Anthony when he said he hadn't seen Rex in a while, but they had nothing else to go on. They should at least see the "ferocious beast" Mrs Partridge had described.

"Can we see him?" Rowan asked. He knew it sounded strange, so he quickly added, "With all these dogs going missing, we want to make sure he's okay."

Anthony gave him a weird look but said, "I guess that's fine. Be quick, though. I'm on my break and don't want to be late getting back to work."

Astrid and Rowan walked quickly towards the house. When Astrid realised Quinn and Jace weren't joining them, she asked, "You guys coming?"

Jace and Quinn looked at each other. Jace said, "That's okay, we'll stay here."

Quinn quickly nodded her head and added, "Yeah, it sounds more like a two-person job."

Astrid shook her head and laughed. "Wimps."

Rowan and Astrid followed Anthony into the house. As the three of them stood in the hall, Anthony called out, "Duke! Come here, boy!"

They waited a few seconds, but no dog appeared. For a moment Rowan was worried that maybe all the dogs of Somerville *were* going missing.

"Lazy dog," Anthony grumbled under his breath. He called over his shoulder to Rowan and Astrid as he walked towards the back of the house, "Follow me."

The three of them walked into a den off the kitchen. There, lying in a patch of sun on the floor, was an ancient-looking basset hound with large, sad eyes. He let out a large yawn while he stretched and rolled onto his back, his tail wagging lazily and tongue hanging out.

"Hey, Duke," Anthony said as he knelt to rub the old dog's belly.

The words "ferocious beast" were spinning around Rowan's head. What was Mrs Partridge talking about? "How old is Duke?" he asked. "Does he get along with other dogs?"

Rowan knew he was pushing it with all the questions, but was hoping to get some information.

"I don't know how old exactly. Maybe ten?" Anthony said. "I don't know how he gets along with other dogs. He hasn't been to the dog park in ages. The most exercise he gets now is following the patch of sun as it moves across the floor."

Rowan and Astrid were stumped. They didn't want to waste any more of Anthony's time, so they said goodbye and showed themselves out.

Outside, Jace and Quinn were sitting under a shady tree on the front lawn. "Any luck?" Jace asked, stretching.

"Nope," Astrid replied glumly and told them about sweet old Duke.

"That dog wouldn't hurt a fly," Rowan said. "Literally. There was a fly buzzing around him the whole time, and he didn't even notice it."

"I'm pretty sure Mrs Partridge was talking in her sleep. I don't see how Duke could have anything to do with Rex's disappearance," Astrid frowned.

The foursome sat quietly for a moment, no one knowing what to do next.

"Well, we can't just sit here on the Larsens' lawn all day," Jace finally said, standing up. "I'm getting a little hungry. Why don't we go to my house and get something to eat. We can figure out what to do next from there."

Quinn, Rowan and Astrid all froze. Could they actually go to the Potters' place? How could they tell their new friend that they thought his house might be haunted?

"Uh, yeah, sure," Rowan managed to say. "Sounds . . . fun." He looked at Quinn and Astrid for support.

When they didn't say anything at first, he glared in their direction.

"Yeah, sounds good," Quinn finally said weakly.

"Cool," Jace said and walked ahead.

Rowan, Quinn and Astrid all exchanged looks of utter terror as they headed towards the most legendary house in Somerville.

CHAPTER EIGHT

The Potters' place was all the way across town. Rowan, Astrid and Quinn each walked as slowly as they possibly could, unsure about what they were getting themselves into. With his long legs and quick pace, Jace walked ahead of the group the entire way, talking about the search for Mrs Partridge's dog, Rex.

"And what's the deal with her sending us to the Larsens'?" Jace asked over his shoulder to the others. "I agree with Astrid that she was talking in her sleep."

Jace seemed oblivious to the fact that his three new friends were following like zombies behind him. As if being marched to their certain death, Rowan, Quinn and Astrid dragged their feet and fell farther and farther behind, mumbling random responses as Jace kept talking about the search for Rex.

Next, Jace launched into a soliloquy on how the doughnut he'd eaten at Mick's Diner was the best thing he'd ever tasted. Rowan took the opportunity to slow the girls down and drop a bit farther behind.

"What are we doing?" he whispered frantically.

"What does it look like we're doing?" Astrid hissed back. "We're heading to a haunted house. I can't believe you got us into this." She looked equal parts frightened and furious.

Rowan smirked. "Funny how this morning you thought it would be so great to go to the Potters' place, and now look who's scared."

Astrid glared at her brother. "I never said that. You were the one who said it would be cool to live there. I said there are probably ghosts living in the attic."

Teasing his sister helped him feel less afraid. "You're such a baby," he said, shaking his head.

Astrid lunged at Rowan, and Quinn stepped in between to stop them before the pair ended up wrestling on the ground.

"Stop it, you two," Quinn warned. She kept a hand on each of them so they wouldn't start fighting, something she'd witnessed many times. Some days it felt like they'd bicker about anything.

Jace, who was unaware of the shenanigans going on behind him, briefly glanced over his shoulder and said, "You know what I mean?"

The trio hadn't been paying any attention to what Jace had been saying, but Quinn quickly responded, "Of course," and Jace kept talking.

Quinn turned her attention back to Astrid and Rowan and whispered, "I don't see how we get out of this without either telling him the house he just moved into might be haunted or going there and seeing what it's like. Who knows? It might be kind of cool."

"Or we may never be heard from again," Astrid grumbled. "I say we tell him about the Potters' place. I'd want to know if I had moved into a haunted house, wouldn't you? There's got to be something to the rumours. Why else has the house been abandoned this whole time? It must be so creepy and gross inside."

"I'm sure there's nothing wrong with the house," Rowan said uncertainly. He then added, "Besides, what can he do about it if there is? He doesn't seem afraid, and if we tell him it, might freak him out unnecessarily. He might even think we're being idiots and trying to scare him away."

As he said it, he realised that this thought scared him more than going to the Potters' place.

"I say we check it out, and if it seems dodgy we'll tell him about the house's history and get out of there right away," Quinn suggested. Astrid and Rowan nodded in agreement.

"So, what's the secret?" Jace asked. The three of them hadn't noticed that Jace had stopped walking so that they could catch him up. He had a bright smile on his unsuspecting face.

"Secret?" Astrid managed to croak out.

"Is there a secret ingredient?" Jace asked.

Rowan, Astrid and Quinn were puzzled. If Jace knew they were keeping something from him, why was he asking about ingredients?

"In the doughnuts," Jace finally said. "Seriously, I've eaten a lot of doughnuts, and the ones at Mick's Diner are by far the best."

"Ohhhh!" Rowan, Astrid and Quinn practically shouted in unison, relieved that Jace hadn't heard them talking about his potentially haunted house.

Astrid quickly covered, saying, "Well if we told you what it was, it wouldn't be a secret, now would it?"

"I suppose so," Jace said, letting out a laugh.

For a moment, the three of them stood on the road in front of the Potters' place. There were no pavements, since it was the only house around. Visitors had to climb an unwelcoming one hundred steps to get to the house.

"Here we are," Jace said, and the foursome began the ascent.

The Potters' place was not your typical house in more ways than one. When it was first built, it was a simple two-storey house. As the family became larger and grew away from the town, they added on to the original structure to accommodate their growing numbers, rather than building separate houses. They must have enjoyed keeping the extended family under one roof. Rumour had it that almost twenty members of the Potter family were living in the home before they all disappeared.

Astrid tilted her head back to take in the entire house – all three storeys of it. It was a hodgepodge of different types of wood, stones and bricks, as if each generation that added on to the house had found a better material with which to build. Despite these inconsistencies, the house came together in a beautifully odd way. It featured two turrets on the front side and a massive wraparound porch. It was the kind of house Mrs Vega would say had character.

Astrid whispered to Quinn, "It's actually a pretty awesome-looking house."

They climbed the final steps onto the porch and approached the huge double doors.

"Oh, no!" Jace said, making the other three jump a little. "I forgot my key."

Quinn smiled at Astrid, who wiggled her eyebrows as she smiled back.

"Oh, well, we tried," Astrid said and headed down the porch steps.

"We'll have to come back another time," Quinn said, following quickly behind Astrid.

"Hang on," Jace called. "I forget my keys all the time. This isn't even the first time I've forgotten them since we moved in two weeks ago. I found another way we can get in without them."

"Oh, great," Astrid mumbled under her breath.

They walked around to the side of the house and stopped at the cellar door.

"Pull on that side," Jace instructed to Rowan as he grabbed a handle and lifted one side. Rowan pulled the other to reveal a set of steps that led down to what must have been the basement.

"The door to the basement doesn't lock all the way. All you have to do is shove it and it pops open," Jace informed them. "I can go in here, and I'll come around and open the front door for you. The basement is pretty gross. You probably don't want to see it."

No one argued. The thought of the Potters' basement petrified Rowan, Quinn and Astrid. Jace didn't seem the least bit afraid. "Meet you in front," he called as he trotted down the steps.

The trio walked in silence to the front of the house. After what felt like an eternity, they finally heard footsteps on the other side of the door.

"Here goes nothing," Astrid said quietly as Jace swung open the giant front door.

They were shocked as they walked in. None of them expected what they saw inside.

CHAPTER NINE

"Whoa," was all Rowan could manage to say as they walked into the Potters' place. It was more than Astrid and Quinn could manage, though, because they were too stunned to speak at all.

While the doors to the Potters' place were massive, decrepit pieces of weather-beaten wood, the inside of the house gleamed and was shiny and modern. The high ceiling and bright, open space had the feeling of a luxurious hotel, rather than a one-hundred-year-old home in Somerville.

The floors were a highly polished dark wood that stretched through the room and beyond. Rugs of different sizes and shapes woven in rich tones were artfully placed and broke the room into gathering spaces. The walls were painted in warm colours that helped create a welcoming and comfortable feel.

At the far end of the large room was a kitchen, and to the right of the front door was an enormous staircase with an intricate pattern of tiny flowers and vines climbing up the wooden banister that curved up to the second floor.

"Whoa," Rowan said again.

Jace smiled proudly. He bowed and said, "Welcome to *mi casa*."

Astrid regained her voice and said, "Wait, when was this place renovated? There is no way it looked like this when the Potters lived here." She pointed to the big flat-screen TV hanging above the stone fireplace as further proof.

"Um, well, I don't know." Jace shrugged. "It was like this when we moved in. Let's hit the kitchen. I'm starving."

Astrid began to object, but Rowan grabbed her arm and pulled her into the kitchen. She glared at him and let out an "Ouch!" when he gave her arm an extra squeeze.

Jace led them into the kitchen at the back of the house, which was as modern and beautiful as the rest of the first floor. Shiny appliances of all shapes and sizes covered the countertops, ready to prepare any meal imaginable. In the corner stood an enormous fridge, on the front of which was a large screen.

"Is that a computer screen on your fridge? Now I know *that* wasn't around when the Potters lived here, and as far as I know, no one else has lived here since," Astrid said as she looked around the room.

"Stop it," Rowan warned her under his breath. He went to covertly grab her arm again, but she ducked around the massive granite-covered island in the middle of the room and out of his grasp just in time.

She continued her line of questioning. "And when was all this work done? People are so nosy in Somerville. How did all this get done without anybody knowing? People definitely would have talked about this."

Jace was facing the huge double-door fridge and had his back to the others. He kept quiet for a moment before slumping his shoulders and letting out a deep sigh.

Astrid, Quinn and Rowan held their breath and exchanged looks. Somehow the strangest house in Somerville had become even more mysterious than they originally thought, and it looked like their new friend might fill them in on how that was possible.

Jace turned slowly to face them. He took another deep breath and said, "Here's the thing ..."

"Hello!" a voice called from the hall, causing Astrid, Rowan and Quinn to almost jump out of their skins. "Is that you, Jace?"

"In the kitchen," Jace called back. It was hard to tell if he was relieved or annoyed by the interruption.

They heard footsteps come down the hall, and a few seconds later Evie walked into the kitchen carrying a shopping bag. She looked surprised to find Rowan, Astrid and Quinn there.

"Oh!" she said, startled. "Hi, guys." She turned towards Jace, adding, "I didn't know you had company."

Evie pursed her lips into a tight frown as she glared at Jace, clearly upset that he had invited people into the house. Jace didn't appear worried. He grabbed the bag of shopping from her arm and began rummaging through it.

"Did you get anything good to eat?" he asked as he pulled out a loaf of bread along with some bananas, strawberries and a container of yogurt.

"It's all good stuff," Evie replied in a snippy tone. In a quieter voice, she added, "Jace, can I talk to you for a moment?"

Jace moved into the pantry in hopes of finding something to eat. "Sure. What's up?" he said casually.

Evie walked into the pantry. Pulling on Jace's arm, she snapped, "In private."

"Okay, fine," Jace said as the pair headed out of the kitchen and down the hallway.

"Yikes," Quinn mouthed to Rowan and Astrid. They nodded their heads in agreement. The three of them were still shell-shocked by all that they had seen in their visit to the Potters' place. They stood in stunned silence as they tried to sort it all out.

The silence didn't last long, though, as Jace's voice came from the hallway.

"Because they're my friends," he told his mum. She must have told him off him for raising his voice, because the next thing they heard was Jace saying, "I will not lower my voice! They are my friends and if I want to have them here, I will."

Astrid raised her eyebrows and whispered, "Double yikes."

Rowan shushed her as a look of concern crossed his face. He felt awful that their visit had gotten Jace into trouble.

For a few moments they could hear the pair fighting, but they couldn't make out what they were saying. Their voices escalated, however, as the argument grew more heated. It became impossible not to listen.

"Listen, Evie, you can't tell me what to do," Jace said. Rowan, Astrid and Quinn exchanged disbelieving looks. Did Jace just call his mum by her first name?

"Oh, yes I can," Evie responded. "And if you don't listen to me, he'll find out and we'll be moving away from here in the blink of an eye. Is that what you want?"

"No!" Jace shouted.

The shouting stopped and an eerie silence came over the room. Rowan, Astrid and Quinn stood motionless. A moment later they heard footsteps coming down the hall. Quinn and Astrid struck up a conversation in an effort to make it appear as though they hadn't heard the pair fighting.

"Some weather we're having," Quinn stated a bit too loudly.

"Sunny and warm. Not a cloud in the sky," Astrid said, a little too enthusiastically.

Jace entered the kitchen alone. He rubbed at his eyes, which were red and glassy. Astrid and Quinn gave up their lame attempt at acting natural. No one knew what to say. As much as they wanted to know what was going on, they could tell by the look on Jace's face that now wasn't the time to ask. All three of them wanted to help Jace, but didn't know how.

Rowan finally broke the silence by saying, "We'd better get going."

"That's right," Quinn added immediately. "I've got a piano lesson tonight."

"And we've got to help Mum and Dad at the restaurant," Astrid said, heading towards the door.

Jace didn't argue. He stood by himself, sadly staring at the floor.

Quinn and Astrid said their goodbyes and left quickly. Rowan stood in the doorway a moment longer. He didn't want to leave with Jace so upset. "So, we'll pick up the search for Rex tomorrow?" Rowan asked.

Jace kept his eyes down and mumbled, "I don't know, maybe."

"Hey!" Rowan had a great idea. "Why don't we meet at the restaurant in the morning? I'll be sure to set a few doughnuts aside for you." He lightly punched Jace on the arm before adding, "I know how much you love them."

Jace looked up. With a small, grateful smile on his face he said, "Sounds good. See you tomorrow."

CHAPTER TEN

Even though she was the baker of the most delicious doughtnuts in Somerville and beyond, Mrs Vega was a health nut at heart. She was always trying to put a healthy spin on the restaurant's most popular recipes. Some of these twists were well received and had increased business at the restaurant. Others had failed miserably. Even with the failures, Mrs Vega was not deterred and kept trying new things.

"Who wants to try some fresh brownies right out of the oven?" she called as she walked out from the kitchen holding a tray of treats.

"Me!" Astrid said as she raced towards her mum.

"Brownies for breakfast? Great idea," Mr Vega said as he wrapped an arm around his wife's shoulder and grabbed a brownie from the tray with his free hand.

It was early in the morning, the day after the kids had visited the Potters' place, and the family was getting ready to open the restaurant. Rowan was the last one to take a brownie, and he did so with a skeptical look on his face. Was his mum really giving them brownies for breakfast?

"Ew, gross!" Astrid said as she spat out her bite of brownie into a napkin.

"Astrid! Where are your manners?" her mother scolded. She turned towards Mr Vega for backup and caught him as he raised a napkin to his mouth to do the very thing that had got his daughter into trouble. He smiled sheepishly at his wife, lowered the napkin and swallowed his bite with a loud gulp.

"New recipe?" he asked tentatively, reaching for a glass of water.

Rowan placed his uneaten brownie back down on the tray with a thud and said, "No, thanks."

"Oh, come on, guys. They taste just like normal brownies but have no sugar," Mrs Vega pleaded. "None at all."

"That's the only difference?" Astrid asked. "Some of your other sugar-free recipes are delicious." She screwed up her face and pointed towards the tray, adding, "But those brownies are nasty."

"Well . . ." Mrs Vega began. "I may have added some shredded vegetables as well."

"No sugar *and* you added vegetables?" Astrid asked in disbelief. "No, thank you."

Mrs Vega watched as her husband drained his second glass of water to get what must have been an awful taste from his mouth. "Too much healthy for one brownie?" she asked him.

"Way too much," he said, looking around. He grabbed a doughnut and shoved half of it into his mouth. He smiled and, with his mouth full of sweetness, said, "Stick to doughnuts."

"Oh!" Rowan said. "Speaking of doughnuts, will you set some aside for Jace? He's obsessed with them and I told him I'd save him a couple."

"You bet," Mr Vega said, placing a few doughnuts on a plate and setting it under the counter. "That Jace seems pretty nice, huh?" he asked.

"Yeah, he's really cool," Rowan said.

Astrid was less enthusiastic, saying vaguely, "He's okay."

Rowan shot Astrid a look, but before Mr Vega could question her lukewarm response, the door opened and the morning regulars began filing into the restaurant.

Astrid and Rowan were on dish duty that morning, so they retreated to the kitchen as the first guests were being served. They immediately began discussing the previous day's drama as they filled the giant sink with soapy hot water.

Astrid began, "What I don't understand is how they made that big old scary house look so amazing.

That had to be a lot of work, and how did they do it without anyone in town seeing? How could they afford it? When they moved to town, Evie didn't even have a job."

Rowan thought for a moment. "Maybe it has something to do with Jace's dad. Maybe he's rich and paid for everything."

"Maybe," Astrid pondered the idea. "But where is he? Has Jace even mentioned his dad to you?"

"He mentioned something about going to a bike race with him, but that was it," Rowan told her, thinking hard. He suddenly remembered how Jace's mood had shifted when he'd mentioned his dad, but decided not to tell that to Astrid. "Maybe his mum or dad is a professional cyclist, and they travel the world racing? That would explain where the money came from."

"Maybe," Astrid said again, although she looked doubtful. "Don't you think that's something he would have mentioned? I know I would have if our dad was a professional bike rider who made lots of money."

Rowan shrugged. "I don't know. Jace seems pretty private, not like someone who would boast."

Astrid couldn't argue with that, so she decided to move on. "And what about that weird fight between Jace and his mum? Why didn't she want us there? It wasn't like we were doing anything. And who was it they were worried about finding out and making them move again? Plus, didn't you think it was weird when Jace called her 'Evie'? That was just crazy."

Rowan was annoyed with Astrid's dramatic spin on the situation. He knew something strange was going on, but he wanted to believe the best of his new friend. It had upset him when Evie mentioned moving away, and he worried that their prying into Jace and Evie's business would make that happen.

"Kids do that all the time," he snapped. "Stop being so dramatic."

Astrid stopped drying the plate she was holding and stared at her brother like he had three heads. "Are you seriously going to pretend like this whole thing isn't totally bizarre? First, Jace and Evie move to town totally unannounced and live in Somerville's creepiest house, which has been completely renovated without anyone noticing. Then they get into a strange fight and she threatens to move away if some mystery man finds out Jace had some friends over. Not to mention the fact that Mrs Partridge's dog suddenly goes missing when they show up."

Rowan angrily threw the cup he had been washing back into the water. "Now you're going to blame Jace for stealing Rex?" he shouted. "That's totally ridiculous. Why would he spend the day helping us find him? Where would he keep him? We were in his house! And why would he even steal him in the first place? You've lost your mind." Hot, soapy water flew up around Rowan as he angrily washed.

As soon as she had said it, Astrid knew that implying Jace had stolen Rex was a bad idea. She hated to lose an argument with her brother, though, so she shouted back, "Something is up with those two and you know it. We might not know what it is, but it doesn't take a genius to notice it."

Just then Mr Vega came into the room, carrying a large stack of dirty dishes. "Hey, hey!" he said. "What's all the shouting about?"

"Nothing," Astrid and Rowan mumbled at the same time, shooting each other dirty looks.

Mr Vega noticed and asked, "Are you two sure everything is all right?"

Things definitely weren't right, but Rowan and Astrid each nodded and went back to cleaning the dishes in silence.

CHAPTER ELEVEN

The morning rush was winding down as Chester Feeney, Marcus Sloane and Miss Coco sat at the counter of Mick's Diner. Chester and Marcus had shut down the garage for a late breakfast, and Miss Coco was enjoying a cheese Danish and a refill on her morning cup of coffee.

"I'm pretty sure New Mexico is part of the United States, Miss Coco," Marcus said respectfully, trying to stifle a chuckle. For a second, though, he doubted himself and turned towards Chester for confirmation. "Isn't that right, Chester?"

Being older and wiser than Marcus, and having had more than one inane conversation with Miss Coco over the years, Chester shoved a mouthful of hash browns into his mouth and shrugged. He kept his eyes on his plate, staying out of their wacky conversation.

"But it's got 'Mexico' right in the name," Miss Coco argued. "If it was part of the United States, why didn't they call it 'New United State'?"

Without Chester's confirmation, Marcus was feeling flustered. "I, uh, I don't know? Maybe because it's down near Mexico?"

"Oh, for Pete's sake," Chester said under his breath. All of this nonsense was ruining his breakfast. He took one last bite of his meal, wiped his mouth with a napkin, cleared his throat and asked, "So, Miss Coco, I hear you've taken up bird-watching? Tell me more about it."

"Oh, yes," Miss Coco began. If she was bothered by the change of topic, she didn't show it. She loved talking about her latest hobby. "Just the other day I saw a red-breasted nuthatch. A little-known fact about the nuthatch is . . ."

As Miss Coco went on and on about her bird-watching, Marcus smiled gratefully at Chester. Chester nodded and shot Marcus a look that said, *You owe me one.*

Just then the restaurant door chimed, and in walked Evie and Jace. Marcus remembered Evie very well from the first time she had walked into the restaurant. Suddenly he'd forgotten all about the maddening conversation with Miss Coco.

"Hi there, Evie," he called cheerfully.

Evie smiled shyly as her cheeks turned a light shade of pink. "Hi," she said.

"I don't know if you remember me or not. I'm Marcus and I run Earl's Petrol Station across the street. This is Chester," he said, poking his thumb in Chester's direction. "He works there with me."

"Welcome to Somerville," Chester said politely.

"And I am Mrs Coretta Lownie," Miss Coco said with great formality.

Evie smiled and said, "I know, Miss Coco. We met the first time I came in. I work here now." Miss Coco looked unsure, so Evie went on. "Remember yesterday, when we talked for a half hour about your bunions?"

"Oh, my bunions are just killing me," Miss Coco said, ending her conversation about birds and proceeding to talk about her sore feet in great detail.

Jace listened to the gory details with wide eyes. He was more than a little relieved when Rowan and Astrid appeared from the back of the restaurant.

"What's up?" Rowan said in an overly enthusiastic tone. He was trying to act normal and welcoming, as if the weird events of the previous day had never happened, but he could tell that he was failing miserably. He hoped that Jace didn't notice.

"'Sup?" Jace replied as the two did an intricate handshake flawlessly, as if they'd known each other their whole lives.

There was a very brief, awkward silence before Rowan smiled and said, "I had my dad set aside some doughnuts for you. Let me grab them."

Rowan and Jace went to the end of the counter. The awkwardness Rowan had felt began to disappear as the pair sat munching on doughnuts.

"I really hope we can find Rex," Rowan said, selecting a second doughnut. "Mrs Partridge loves that silly dog."

"She sure does," Jace agreed. "Sometimes big dogs freak me out. I'm just glad we're looking for a little dog."

"Yeah, and not a hamster," Rowan said. As soon as he said it, his cheeks flushed red and he looked up at Jace with wide eyes.

Jace let out a laugh. "Are you saying you're afraid of hamsters?"

"Well, uh, um, not *every* hamster," Rowan muttered, looking away from Jace.

"Just *some* hamsters?" Jace asked, trying his best to hold back his laughter.

After a moment, Rowan let out a deep sigh. "Quinn used to have this hamster called Mr Snuggles. It was all white with beady red eyes and really sharp teeth. The one time I tried to hold him, he bit me. I dropped him, and we couldn't find him for over an hour. I kept seeing him out of the corner of my eye and thought he was going to crawl up my leg." Rowan shivered at the memory. "Hamsters are just plain creepy."

"I can see how that would freak you out," Jace said as he nodded his head. He tried to keep a straight face as he added, "Are you afraid of all small animals, or just hamsters?"

Rowan shook his head. "I don't even know why I just told you that. I've never told anyone, not even Astrid."

"You told me because we're friends," Jace began. "And you should never, ever, tell Astrid. She'll never stop teasing you."

Rowan relaxed and laughed. "No kidding."

Astrid was frustrated as she watched her brother and Jace laughing at the end of the counter. She knew

Jace was hiding something and didn't understand why her brother couldn't see that. She liked Jace but thought that she would feel better when she knew the whole story, and she was determined to find it out.

"Hi, Jace," Astrid said coolly as she walked towards the end of the counter.

"Hi, Astrid," Jace said with a bright smile.

How annoying! Astrid thought. *Why did he have to be so nice*?

"Are you ready to find a dog today?" Jace asked as he reached for another doughnut.

"Let's hope so," Astrid replied. "I talked to Quinn this morning, and she said Mrs Partridge called her dad loads of times last night. She said she was too sad to sleep without Rex."

"That's awful," Jace said.

Astrid nodded. "I know. Quinn will be here any minute, and then we can figure out where to look next."

Just then Quinn burst through the door of Mick's Diner. Her eyes raced as she searched for her friends, among the booths. When she spotted them she dashed over.

She was out of breath as if she had run the entire way to the restaurant. She put her hands on her knees and blurted out, "Rex came home today."

"That's great," Astrid said.

Quinn shook her head and took a deep breath in before adding, "Mrs Partridge said his fur was filthy and his paws and snout were stained red. It looked like he'd been bleeding."

CHAPTER TWELVE

Rowan, Astrid and Jace shouted goodbyes to their parents and bolted out of Mick's, with Quinn leading the way.

As they headed towards Mrs Partridge's house, Rowan said to Quinn, "Tell us everything you know."

"I was getting ready to leave this morning when my dad said he was going to stop by Mrs Partridge's on his way to the office. She must have called him a million times last night and was still really upset," Quinn said. "I thought I would go with him to see if I could find out anything that might help us today."

"Good thinking," Jace replied.

Quinn smiled at Jace. Like Astrid, Quinn wasn't sure what to think about Jace after the strange visit to the Potters' place the day before. But she still thought Jace was a nice guy and hoped that all the odd happenings could be explained.

"Thanks," she said sincerely, before continuing her story. "So, when we got there, Mrs Partridge was in the same spot on the couch as when we left her yesterday. She looked awful, like she hadn't slept all night. My dad tried to calm her down. We must have left the front door open because the next thing I knew, I heard Rex barking in the doorway."

"Barking?" Astrid interrupted. "I thought he was covered in blood and half-dead?"

Quinn tried not to roll her eyes at her best friend's dramatic tendencies. "That's not what I said," she said. "I *said* he was covered in blood – which he was – but I never said he was dying. In fact, my dad checked him over and said that he seemed perfectly fine and didn't have a scratch on him."

Rowan asked, "If he was perfectly fine, then where did the blood come from?"

"My dad and I couldn't figure it out. We cleaned him, and then my dad headed to work. After all the calls last night, I think he was just as relieved as Mrs Partridge," Quinn said.

"How is Mrs Partridge?" Jace asked.

"She seemed happy but, as you can imagine, she's very confused. As soon as Rex was clean, he ran to the door and started barking. When we left, he tried to get out again," Quinn said. "I know Rex is home, but I still think there is more to this story that we need to figure out."

"This town is full of mysteries lately," Astrid said, looking at Jace.

Rowan gave his sister a dirty look before saying, "I agree, Quinn. Let's go see what we can find out at Mrs Partridge's."

At Mrs Partridge's flat, Rowan, Jace, Quinn and Astrid were surprised when Captain Joel Osgood of the Somerville Police Department answered the door.

"Is everything okay?" Rowan asked anxiously.

Captain Osgood sighed. "About as good as can be expected."

Joel Osgood was a lifelong resident of Somerville, having only left to serve in the Army for three years after leaving high school. He returned to Somerville a respected veteran and went to college before quickly working his way up the ranks of the Somerville Police Department. He was the youngest person to ever become captain.

When Captain Osgood opened the door a bit further, they saw Delilah Doherty and Mrs Partridge standing with their arms crossed, glaring at each other. Mrs Partridge held a lead, and at the other end Rex strained towards the door.

Captain Osgood shuffled them in quickly and shut the door behind them. In a quiet voice he explained, "Mrs Partridge called and said there was an emergency, and when I got here she told me that Delilah had hurt Rex. I asked Delilah to come over so we could get to the bottom of this mess, but so far it isn't going well."

Once they understood what was going on, Astrid said, "We're so glad Rex came back, Mrs Partridge."

"I was, too," Mrs Partridge responded. Then, without taking her eyes off Delilah, she added, "But whoever took him must have done something awful to him. He's been trying to get back out ever since he got home. Someone who would mistreat a dog like that should be run out of town."

The usually mild-tempered Delilah had reached the end of her patience. "For the last time, I did not steal your dog."

Captain Osgood put his hand on Delilah's arm. She let out a deep breath as her shoulders relaxed. In fact, Quinn and Astrid noticed a small smile cross Delilah's face as she looked at Captain Osgood.

Captain Osgood kept his hand on Delilah's arm a moment longer before saying, "Mrs Partridge, I've done a thorough investigation, and there is nothing that links Delilah to Rex's disappearance. It appears that Rex somehow got out for a little while, but thankfully he came back home."

Mrs Partridge frowned and crossed her arms tighter. Under her breath she muttered, "I still think she should close down that awful sweet shop."

Rowan remembered Mrs Partridge making a similar statement about Delilah closing down her shop when Rex had first gone missing. In all the chaos, he hadn't thought to question it at the time, but now asked, "Mrs Partridge, why do you want Delilah to close down her shop?"

Mrs Partridge looked surprised, as if she hadn't realised she had made that last statement out loud. She mumbled, "Well, it's just, well, because she stole my dog, and that's why."

Delilah pressed Mrs Partridge. "Why do you really want me to close down? Ever since it opened, I've tried to be a good neighbour, and now you're accusing me of stealing your beloved dog. It doesn't make sense."

Mrs Partridge sank down into her chair. As if sensing his owner's sadness, Rex stopped trying to get out the door and hopped onto Mrs Partridge's lap. He licked her face before curling up in a ball.

Mrs Partridge let out a deep sigh. "It's just that most folks who stop in Somerville only have time for a few stops. They usually get petrol, a bite to eat at Mick's and stop at one or two other places. Ever since your shop opened, everyone goes there instead of the museum. My business has been cut almost in half."

Delilah crossed the room and knelt down in front of Mrs Partridge. "I'm so sorry, I had no idea. I never meant to take away your business. I thought since my business had been so good, so had yours."

Mrs Partridge frowned and shook her head. "Well, it hasn't," she mumbled.

The room was silent for a moment. Then Delilah stood up quickly. "Hey, I've got an idea. Maybe I could set up a little display in my shop – somewhere near the till so customers see it when they pay – to promote the museum. I can tell people about all of the great things to see at the museum and suggest they stop in."

"You would do that?" Mrs Patridge asked.

Delilah nodded. "Of course I would. I can even supply you with some of my new lollipops to give out to kids who come in."

Mrs Partridge's eyes widened. "That would be delicious, er, I mean, delightful."

"I've taken a lot of marketing classes," Delilah said as she began pacing with excitement. "I bet I could come up with some great ideas to drive traffic to the museum."

Mrs Partridge raised her hand to stop her. "Oh, no, the sweets and the display will be plenty. I don't want the museum to get *too* busy. I still want to be able to shut down for a couple of hours for my afternoon nap, and I hate having to kick people out."

Delilah smiled. "I'm sorry that my shop caused you trouble at the museum."

Mrs Partridge reached out and took Delilah's hand. "Don't be. I just love that place so much. I got scared

I was going to have to close, and instead of doing something about it, I blamed you. I'm so sorry that I accused you of taking my beloved Rex."

When he heard his name, Rex jumped up and off Mrs Partridge's lap. He raced for the door and began scratching at it and barking.

"I still don't know why that dog is acting so strangely," Mrs Partridge said. "I'm worried he's going to get out again."

"He seems very determined to go somewhere," Captain Osgood noted.

Jace spoke up. "What do you think about us taking him out on his lead? Maybe he'll lead us to where he was all night."

Mrs Partridge protested, "Oh, I don't think so. Seeing him covered in blood this morning was just awful."

Rex continued to bark and spin in circles at the door. "What if I went with the kids, Mrs Partridge?" Captain Osgood offered. "It would be nice to figure out what is going on with your dog."

Mrs Partridge reluctantly agreed, and the foursome, plus Captain Osgood, headed out the door, with Rex leading the way.

"Now we know why Mrs Partridge had it in for Delilah," Rowan commented. "At least one mystery's been solved."

Astrid shot a look in Jace's direction before adding, "Oh, there are plenty of mysteries left to be solved."

CHAPTER THIRTEEN

Rex darted out the door, and even though the five of them were walking at a brisk pace, he strained against his collar, urging them to move more quickly.

"He certainly seems to know where he's going," Astrid commented. She was doing her best to hold onto Rex's lead as she and Quinn moved ahead of the group at the little dog's insistence.

Not much got by the head of the Somerville Police Department, and even though he knew about Evie and Jace moving to town, he had yet to meet them. He turned towards Jace and extended his hand saying, "I don't think we've met yet. I'm Captain Joel Osgood. Welcome to Somerville."

Jace smiled shyly and shook Captain Osgood's hand. "Thanks, I'm Jace."

Ever the detective, Captain Osgood asked, "Where did you move here from?"

Rowan saw a look of discomfort cross Jace's face but decided not to help his friend out as he had before. He, too, wanted to find out where Jace and Evie were from, but it seemed that wasn't going to happen.

"Out East," Jace said, giving Captain Osgood his standard vague response.

Captain Osgood nodded and didn't ask for further details. Rowan was frustrated but also relieved that Rex had pulled Astrid and Quinn out of earshot.

Up ahead, Rex pulled Astrid off the pavement and into the alley next to Goodwin's Market. Although

Astrid had been holding on with both hands, Rex pulled with all his might and was able to break free from her grasp. They all ran to chase the dog behind the market and watched as he climbed an arrangement of empty boxes that served as a staircase up the side of a huge wheelie bin. When he reached the top, however, Rex appeared frustrated and barked and growled as he scratched at the lid.

Just then a voice came from the grocery store's back door. "I already told you to go away."

As the group got closer, they saw that the owner of that voice was Anthony Larsen, the same boy they had questioned the day before about his ancient dog, Duke.

Anthony looked startled when he saw them approach. "Oh, hi, guys." He lowered his head slightly and added, "Captain Osgood."

"Hello, Anthony," the captain said.

Anthony wore the expression of someone who had been caught red-handed. He tried diverting their attention by pointing at Rex and saying, "Hey, isn't that the dog you guys were looking for?"

"It is," Captain Osgood said. "He came home this morning."

"What a relief," Anthony said and turned quickly to walk back into the store. "See you around."

"Just a minute, Anthony," the captain said. "I'd like to ask you some questions."

Anthony stopped walking, hung his head and turned around.

Rowan stepped forward and asked excitedly, "Yeah, like what did you mean when you said you'd told Rex to go away already?" He was happy that they were finally getting somewhere with this mystery.

Captain Osgood raised his eyebrows. He was used to taking the lead in such investigations, but he stepped back and let Rowan take over.

"Well, uh, you know, I've seen that dog before," Anthony stalled. He looked between Captain Osgood and Rowan, not sure to whom he should be talking.

Realising that he had spoken out of place, Rowan looked sheepishly at Captain Osgood. Without saying a word, Captain Osgood lifted his hand as if to say, "Go ahead."

Rowan nodded to the captain and then asked Anthony, "When, exactly, was the last time you saw Rex?"

Anthony rubbed the back of his neck and was quiet for a moment, as if he was deciding what he should say next. After another beat, he puffed his cheeks, blew out a deep breath and said quietly, "This morning."

Rowan asked, "Where did you see him?"

Anthony looked at the ground as he answered. "He was in the big wheelie bin when I took out some rubbish this morning. He ran away as soon as I opened the lid."

"Why didn't you let Mrs Partridge know that you'd seen her dog?" Astrid asked, joining in the investigation.

"And why was Rex covered in blood?" Quinn added.

Anthony looked up at the sky, avoiding eye contact with any of them as he confessed, "He must have got into the bin when I was cleaning up at closing time last night. I was in a hurry to get out of here and threw in some of the bloody scraps instead of disposing of them properly. He must have been in there when I closed the lid."

At this point he looked directly at the group. "I didn't know the dog was in there, honest. When I came in this morning and took out some rubbish, he darted out. I thought about calling Mrs Partridge, but when I saw the blood on him I thought my boss would know that I rushed last night and didn't follow procedures. Then he'd never let me close the department again, and I'd lose my promotion. I thought Rex would make his way home and I could keep my job."

Anthony hung his head again, adding sincerely, "I know I messed up. I'm sorry."

"You sure did." Rowan was all fired up as he scolded Anthony. "Poor Mrs Partridge couldn't sleep at all last night."

Captain Osgood took a step forward and said quietly to Rowan, "I'll take it from here."

"Oh, yeah, sure," Rowan said and took a step back, but not before shooting Anthony a mean look.

"I'm really sorry," Anthony repeated again. "I won't do it again."

"That's right, you won't," Captain Osgood said. "We're going to have a little chat with your boss and you're going to tell him everything."

Anthony started to protest, but Captain Osgood kept on talking. "I'll be sure to remind him that you are new to this job and that everyone deserves a second chance, but it's going to be up to you to follow through and start following the procedures."

After Anthony's confession, Quinn had gone over to grab Rex off the bin. She held him tight, but he was still squirming in her arms, hoping to get back into it. "What about Rex?" she asked. "How is Mrs Partridge going to keep him inside, when all he wants to do is get in that bin?"

"He must miss the bones he usually gets at the butcher," Astrid offered. "Anthony said yesterday that he hasn't seen them in a while, and Mrs Partridge said today that they haven't been going on their usual walks."

"I think that as a way of saying he's sorry to Mrs Partridge, Anthony will deliver bones to Rex until Mrs Partridge is feeling up to her walks again. That way, if Rex has them at home, he won't feel the need to get out to get them. What do you think, Anthony?" Captain Osgood asked.

Anthony nodded glumly. "Yes, sir."

"Cheer up," Captain Osgood told Anthony. "It will all work out. Now get Rex a bone to take home, and we'll go talk with your boss."

Rowan, Jace, Astrid and Quinn followed behind Rex as the little dog trotted along happily with a juicy bone in his mouth.

"Wow," Rowan said as he practically skipped down the street. "I can't believe we solved that mystery. Jace, that was such a great idea to see where Rex wanted to go. And when Captain Osgood let me question Anthony like a real detective? That was awesome. I wish we had another mystery to solve."

Astrid cleared her throat and pointed her head in Jace's direction.

Rowan felt himself deflate. He had been so caught up in the excitement he had forgotten about the strange happenings with his new friend at the Potters' place the day before. He knew his sister wasn't going to let it drop and, quite honestly, he wanted to know more about Jace and his mum, too.

"So, Jace, did anything like that ever happen in your old neighbourhood?" Rowan asked.

"No." Jace laughed. "No missing dogs."

Just as Rowan had thought she would, Astrid then asked, "And where exactly is your old neighbourhood?"

Jace looked quickly to Rowan, and when his friend didn't help him out for the second time that day, Jace said quietly, "You know, out East . . ."

Astrid wasn't letting it go that easily. "Where out East? New York? Connecticut? Maine? There are lots of states out East."

Jace stopped walking. He gave a tight smile and said quickly, "Look, it was a lot of fun helping you guys find Rex, but I've got a lot going on, so I'll see you around."

Before the others could say a word, Jace took off running in the direction of the Potters' place. Rowan tried calling out to him, but Jace was long gone.

Rowan turned angrily towards Astrid. "You just had to scare him off, didn't you?"

"I was just trying to find out what is going on," Astrid replied.

"Well, you didn't have to badger him so much. I'm sure he would have told us if we gave him a chance," Rowan said, fuming.

Quinn stepped in between the siblings and said in a calm voice, "Rowan, come on. You've got to admit that something is up with Jace and his mum. Look, I like him, too, but when he can't even tell us where he's from, maybe it's better if we give him some space while he sorts out whatever is going on with him."

Rowan couldn't argue with what Quinn had said, but it didn't make him feel any better. "Whatever," he muttered and walked off.

CHAPTER FOURTEEN

Rowan sat alone at the end of the counter at Mick's Diner. He showed no emotion as he stared blankly at the game he played on his laptop. Besides working in the restaurant, he hadn't moved much from that spot in a few days.

"I'm starting to get worried about him. I think this whole Jace thing is really bothering him," Astrid said to Quinn as the pair sat at the other end of the counter, flipping through magazines. For a moment Quinn was surprised by Astrid's concern for her brother, since the siblings spent most of their time fighting. Before Quinn could comment, though, Astrid went on, "It's so annoying when he's so sulky. It's a total bummer."

"This whole thing is a bummer," Quinn responded. "It was kind of fun when the four of us were hanging out. It was nice to have something to do, and Jace is a pretty cool guy."

"I guess," Astrid shrugged. "But you have to admit that something is up with him. No one has seen him in almost a week. What is he even doing up there by himself at the Potters' place? Why is everything so secretive with him?"

"I don't know," Quinn sighed and flipped shut her magazine. "What I do know is that we aren't even two weeks into the summer holidays and I'm already really bored."

Just then the door opened, and the girls watched as a man they didn't recognise walked into the restaurant. Despite the heat outside, the man wore a black suit that hung loosely on his thin frame. Aside from some close-cropped hair along the side and back of his head, the man was bald and had a large, almost beak-like nose. He certainly didn't look like the usual sort of tourist who stopped in at Mick's.

He sat at the middle of the counter near Miss Coco. Mrs Vega greeted him immediately, saying, "Welcome to Mick's Diner. What can I get for you?"

"Coffee, black," the man said brusquely. "And a few of those doughnuts, please."

"Oh, you'll love those doughnuts," Miss Coco said, turning towards the man. "Some folks say they are the best they've ever had."

The man nodded and gave Miss Coco a tight, dismissive smile. Miss Coco was not one to take a hint, though, and she continued talking. "Say, do I know you? You look awfully familiar to me."

A flash of annoyance crossed the man's face as he responded, "No, ma'am. I'm not from around here. Just passing through."

Miss Coco squinted her eyes and stared at the man. "I'm almost certain I know you. If not you, then someone who looks an awful lot like you."

Mrs Vega set down a plate of doughnuts and tried to save the man from a conversation he obviously didn't want to be a part of by saying, "We get a lot of nice people who pass through here, Miss Coco. I'm sure after a while a few are going to look familiar."

Miss Coco's eyes widened. "I know who you look like. You look like one of the . . ."

Miss Coco was cut short by a loud crash. All eyes turned towards the kitchen door, which Evie had just walked through before dropping a tray of plates. She had recovered quickly, but Astrid and Quinn both saw the look of shock on her face when she saw the man sitting at the counter.

"Oh, my," Mrs Vega said as she went to help Evie clean up. She'd had her back to the kitchen door and didn't see what had caused Evie's accident. The pair cleaned up the mess, with Evie apologising the entire time.

"Don't worry about it," Mrs Vega said sincerely. "You've been working so hard. You're probably exhausted. Why don't you take a little break?"

Evie smiled and nodded her head as Mrs Vega took the tray of broken plates into the kitchen. Evie glanced nervously around the almost-empty restaurant before walking towards the counter.

"That must be my cue to leave," Miss Coco said as she stood up and walked towards the door. "You know what they say, 'It's all fun and games until someone drops a tray of plates.'"

Evie slid into the seat Miss Coco had vacated and, without looking directly at the man, whispered, "What are you doing here?"

Astrid and Quinn picked up their magazines and pretended to be very interested in the latest fashions, even pointing out cute sandals to each other as they strained to eavesdrop on Evie and the mystery man's conversation.

"I could ask you the same thing," the man responded, barely opening his mouth to speak.

They kept talking without looking at each other in voices too low for Astrid and Quinn to hear. Quickly, though, their conversation grew heated and their voices rose a bit.

"Stop threatening me. What are we supposed to do? Stay cooped up in that house?" Evie hissed. "And Jace is a kid. He's going to want to have friends. They've got nothing to do with this."

The man responded curtly, "Perhaps I wasn't clear enough about the level of danger we are talking about here. Like it or not, you must do as I say."

Evie glared at the man one last time before getting up and heading into the ladies' room.

The man gulped his coffee, placed a twenty-dollar note on the counter and abruptly left the restaurant.

Astrid and Quinn exchanged wide-eyed looks before jumping up and racing down to the other end of the counter. Rowan had been engrossed in his game and had missed all the drama. He pulled out an earbud as the girls approached and grunted, "What?"

"We think Jace and his mum are in danger," Quinn

whispered as she glanced anxiously at the ladies' room door. "And I think we might be a part of the problem."

"What are you talking about?" Rowan asked.

Quinn and Astrid quickly filled him in on the conversation they had just overheard. His eyes widened when they got to the part where Evie mentioned Jace's friends.

"Do you think that's the mystery man Evie was talking about when we were at the Potters' place? The one who's going to make them move again?" Rowan asked.

Quinn replied, "It sure sounds that way."

"What do we do now?" Astrid asked.

"I don't know about you two, but I want Jace to stay. I'm going to figure out who this mystery man is and find a way to keep Jace and his mum in Somerville."

Quinn and Astrid exchanged a brief look before proclaiming in unison, "We're in!"

CHAPTER FIFTEEN

Unsure of what to do next, Quinn, Astrid and Rowan agreed that they needed more information. They decided to do some snooping at the Potters' place to try and find clues about the mystery man and why Jace and Evie would have to move.

They knew Evie would be at work until after the dinner rush, and when they overheard her call Jace and tell him to go to Goodwin's Market and "get out of the house and get some fresh air," they decided it was now or never.

They waited across the street from the Potters' place in the opposite direction of the market until they saw Jace heading out. He walked slowly, with his head hung low. Seeing their friend like that motivated them to face their fears of sneaking into the Potters' place.

Once Jace was out of sight, they ran across the street and towards the side of the house. Quinn and Rowan each lifted a side of the door that unveiled the entrance to the basement. For a moment they all stood looking down into the dark, creepy stairwell.

"Are we sure we want to do this?" Quinn asked, saying what they were all thinking.

"Yes," Astrid responded quickly. "Let's go."

Feeling brave, Astrid led the way down the stairs. When she reached the basement door, a mouse darted across her path. She jumped back and let out a yelp. In a flash, all of her certainty about sneaking into the Potters' place vanished. She jiggled the handle and quickly pronounced, "Must be locked. Let's go back to the restaurant and figure out Plan B."

Rowan, who had been annoyed by his sister taking the lead in heading down the stairs, reached around Astrid and gave the door a push. As it popped open he said, "Remember? Jace said you have to shove it open."

"Oh, yeah." Astrid giggled nervously. "I forgot about that part."

The trio crept into the dark and dusty basement. Although Jace had described it as "gross," they found the basement looked much like any other one you'd find in an old house. There were lots of cobwebs and musty-smelling boxes, but there were no skeletons or torture devices to be used on nosy kids, as their wild imaginations might have led them to believe. They stayed close together and quickly made their way to the stairs.

Once they were upstairs, the first floor looked as bright and modern as they had remembered. The only mess was in front of the massive flat-screen TV. Empty crisp bags and video game cases littered the space.

"What now?" Quinn whispered.

"Maybe we should look upstairs?" Rowan suggested.

At the top of the staircase they found a long corridor with doors on both sides and a second set of stairs leading up to the next floor. The first door they tried led in to what appeared to be an office. They hurried in and began looking around.

Quinn checked out the bookshelves, while Rowan and Astrid went to the desk. It was huge and looked like it had been carved out of a single gigantic tree. Although it looked very old, it was solid and sturdy.

Rowan and Astrid were uncomfortable about rifling through someone else's things. They were happy when, after searching through a few file folders, they found something of interest.

"Look at this," Astrid said. She held up a handful of passports. She opened them to reveal different pictures of Jace and Evie with a variety of names and information. The file also contained birth certificates, school transcripts, and driver's licenses with Evie's picture from several states.

"They can become a different person in the blink of an eye," Quinn said.

Astrid added, "Sure makes you wonder who they really are, doesn't it?"

"They're our friends," Rowan barked at this sister. He flipped through the information. "They must have these to run from the mystery man."

Quinn nodded. "Evie did look scared to death when he came in, and she told him to stop threatening her."

"That guy is super creepy," Astrid confirmed.

"Maybe we can find a way to trap him and turn him over to Captain Osgood, so Jace and his mum won't have to run anymore," Rowan said.

"I don't know about capturing him, but I think we definitely need to get Captain Osgood involved," Quinn said.

A nagging thought troubled Astrid. "What if Jace and Evie don't want the police involved? What if they are in some sort of trouble?"

Rowan looked astounded. "You think Jace and Evie are criminals?"

Quinn said quietly, "I hadn't thought of that, but maybe that's why they haven't gone to the police themselves."

"And it would explain why Jace wouldn't tell us anything," Astrid added. "Rowan, I know you and Jace have become friends quickly, but you need to at least keep that open as a possibility."

"I know Jace," Rowan argued. "I may not have known him long, but I think he's a good guy and deserves our help."

When Astrid and Quinn didn't look convinced, he went on, "At the very least let's hear him out. If he can't explain what's going on after we tell him what we've found, then we'll go to Captain Osgood. But if there is anything I can do to help him, I'm going to do it – with or without you."

Rowan turned to storm out of the room but was stopped dead in his tracks. In the doorway stood the mystery man. His arms were crossed, and the expression on his face told Rowan he was not happy to see them.

CHAPTER SIXTEEN

"You must be the pesky kids who are ruining the plan," the mystery man said, shaking his head. "You just had to poke your noses in where they don't belong. I should have known Somerville was a bad idea."

Rowan walked up to the mystery man. "Look, we don't know what's going on, but you need to leave our friend and his mum alone."

"Your friend?" the mystery man said with a laugh. "You don't even know him."

"We know him well enough," Quinn said as she walked over and stood next to Rowan. Rowan gave her a small smile of thanks.

"Oh, really? What has he told you about himself?" the man smirked.

"Well, uh …" Rowan mumbled. Quinn and Astrid scowled in thought.

"That's what I thought," the man said, uncrossing his arms. "Look, do yourselves a favour. Go home and forget about all you saw here. You have no idea of the danger."

"It doesn't matter," Astrid said, joining Rowan and Quinn. "We may not have known Jace long, but we know that he's our friend, and we're going to help him."

Just then Jace appeared from behind the mystery man. He couldn't hide the smile from his face. "Thanks, guys," he said sheepishly. "But what are you doing here?"

"We're trying to figure out what is going on so we can help you," Rowan explained. "We heard you and your mum talking about having to move again, and we want you to stay."

"Then this guy came to town," Astrid said, shooting the mystery man a mean look, "and it seemed like your mum was scared. We thought it might be our fault that he showed up, so we wanted to help protect you."

Jace looked touched. He sighed and said, "Look guys, the truth is –"

"Whoa!" the mystery man cut him off. "Not a good idea. You don't even know these kids. There is no reason for them to know anything more than they already know."

Jace turned to face the mystery man. "The reason they need to know is because they are my friends. They've included me from the minute I got to town."

Jace choked back tears. He took a breath before continuing, "I'd rather be honest with my friends and have to move than stay here and lie to them."

The mystery man shook his head and said, "That's not a good idea."

"Is that a threat?" Astrid asked angrily.

The mystery man looked amused. "Why would I threaten you?"

"We heard you talking to Evie at the restaurant," Quinn said. "We know that you don't want us to be friends with Jace."

"We can call Captain Osgood right now and make sure you never threaten Jace or his mum ever again," Rowan added.

"Slow down there, detective. You may be good at solving mysteries, but you've got this one wrong," Jace said. He put his hand on the mystery man's shoulder. "Mr P is one of the good guys. He's helping us."

"What?" Rowan, Astrid and Quinn exclaimed all at once.

"It's true." Jace chuckled. Then he turned and looked expectantly at the man the kids now knew as Mr P. "See? They're my friends. They deserve to know what's going on. What do you say?"

"They do seem awfully protective of you." Mr P grimaced. He looked at the three confused kids in front of him, then back to Jace. He let out a sigh and said, "Let me make a few calls."

CHAPTER SEVENTEEN

Mick's Diner closed early that night. The sign on the door read, "Sorry for any inconvenience. We'll be back tomorrow morning with a fresh batch of doughnuts."

Amelia and Jason Vega stood talking quietly with Quinn's parents, Brian and Margaret Ramsey, and Captain Osgood. Astrid and Quinn sat together at the counter a few seats down from where Rowan and Jace were sitting. Evie stood nervously on the other side of the counter, drying glasses.

"A little more lemonade over here," Jace said to her with a smirk. Although the pitcher was actually closer to him than to Evie, he held up and jiggled his empty glass to speed her up.

She frowned and spat under her breath, "Get it yourself."

Knowing that he'd be in big trouble if he ever spoke to his mum that way, Rowan looked at Jace and said, "You and your mum sure have an, um, interesting relationship."

Jace laughed. "You have no idea."

Just then the door to Mick's opened, and in walked Mr P. Before anyone could say a thing, he began to speak.

"Thank you all for coming here tonight. My name is Mr P, and I am a senior agent for the National Intelligence Agency."

A gasp arose from the group, but no one said a word.

"I've asked you all here tonight to talk about the two newest residents of Somerville, Jace and Evie. I know people moving to such a small town can cause a lot of speculation, but I assure you, their moving here was not by chance.

"The first thing you need to know is that Jace and Evie's parents are two of our top agents."

Rowan shot Jace a confused look. Jace whispered to him, "See? I've got an annoying sister, too."

Mr P went on, "I can't give you any details, but I can tell you that, unfortunately, Jace and Evie's parents have found themselves in some trouble on a very dangerous mission. For the safety of all involved, we thought it best to send Jace and Evie into hiding. We've tried several cities around the world, and changing their relationship from brother and sister to mother and son, but our sources indicate that so far, no place had been completely secure. I suggested Somerville, and despite the nosiness of some of the residents," Mr P said, looking directly at Quinn, Astrid and Rowan, "it has been by far the most secure location yet. With a town of this size, it was easy to run background checks on all the residents and to monitor any potential threats."

Mr P rolled his eyes slightly before continuing, "And much to my amazement, both Jace and Evie have expressed a desire to stay in Somerville. Turns out they both actually enjoy living here.

"I have asked you all here to bring you up to speed on this situation and to ask for your full cooperation in keeping the details under wraps. I know I am asking a lot, but if you will sign these papers promising your silence, we can keep Jace and Evie here for as long as they, and the town, are safe."

Captain Osgood cleared his throat and said, "I spoke briefly with Mr P this afternoon and with his superior at the agency. I can attest that what he is saying is true and that, while having Jace and Evie as residents of Somerville does not come without its risks, the agency is going above and beyond to keep them, as well as the people of our town, safe. I believe that keeping their identities a secret is best for the town and am comfortable signing the agreement if you all are, too."

"Of course," Mrs Vega said right away. "Whatever we can do to help."

Dr and Mrs Ramsey looked a bit shocked, but both nodded their heads in agreement.

"I still have a question," Astrid said, raising her hand and ignoring her brother's glare. "How did you get the Potters' place to look so nice without anyone knowing?"

For the first time all evening, Mr P looked slightly uncomfortable. "We brought crews in at night."

Astrid raised her hand again, but Mr P put an end to the questions by saying, "Thank you all for your cooperation."

Evie, who hadn't said a word all evening, spoke up. "Jace and I just want to thank you. As you can imagine, it's been a long and stressful year. We miss our parents, and of all the places we've been, we've never felt so cared for and welcomed as we do in Somerville. This truly is an amazing place."

Tears rolled down Evie's face, and Mrs Vega went to her and gave her a huge hug.

"Why don't we celebrate with some doughnuts?" Mr Vega asked.

Rowan noticed a small smile on Mr P's face for the first time all evening. He turned towards Jace and asked, "Is he always so grumpy?"

"Who? Mr P?" Jace laughed. "Yes! But he's really a good guy."

Rowan, Astrid, Jace and Quinn sat together at the counter. Rowan raised his glass of lemonade and said, "To our new friend, Jace, or whatever your real name is."

The group laughed, clinked glasses and took a drink.

Astrid swallowed and immediately raised her glass again. "And here's to many more mysteries for the four of us to solve."

Quinn and Rowan raised their glasses right away, but Jace looked unsure. His three new friends waited and smiled encouragingly at him.

"What the heck?" he said and raised his glass to join the others. "I can't wait to discover the many secrets of Somerville!"

About the Author

Raised in the Chicago suburb of Hoffman Estates in Illinois, USA, Michele Jakubowski has the teachers in her life to thank for her love of reading and writing. While writing has always been a passion for Michele, she believes it is the books she has read throughout the years, and the teachers who assigned them, that have made her the storyteller she is today. Michele lives in Powell, Ohio, with her husband, John, and their children, Jack and Mia.

Glossary

covert secret

decrepit worn out or weakened by old age

deter prevent something or someone

dismissive rejecting someone or something

inane lacking sense

intricate something highly involved or complex

jovial having good humour

passport official booklet that proves that a person is a citizen of a certain country; passports allow people to travel to foreign countries.

petite something of a small size

turret round tower on a building, usually on a corner

vague something not clearly expressed

Examine the Evidence

1. Jace and Evie are supposed to be staying out of the public's eye. What do you think their lives would be like if they never met anyone in Somerville and were stuck inside the Potters' place all the time? Use evidence from the story to support your view.

2. At the end of the book, Jace says he can't wait to solve all the mysteries in Somerville. Does your town or city have a mystery? If not, make one up! Discuss with friends and see who can come up with the best mystery.

3. The restaurant is famous for its delicious doughnuts. But sometimes Mrs Vega's creations don't turn out quite right. What is the most delicious thing you have ever eaten? What foods do you hate? Compare and contrast lists with your friends.

Further Deductions

1. Write a short summary of the conflict between Mrs Partridge and Delilah. Then write about a conflict you have had. How was it similar? How was it different? Was there a resolution?

2. Rewrite the story from Evie's or Jace's perspective. What is Somerville like to a new person? Use details from the text to describe what their move might have been like, and what they might be thinking or feeling.

3. Rowan, Astrid, Jace and Quinn question people in Somerville about Rex's disappearance. Re-read the questions they asked, and then make your own list. What kinds of things might you need to know to find a missing dog? Switch lists with someone else and answer each other's questions.

Solve all the SOMERVILLE Mysteries!

The Sleuths of Somerville
MICK'S BURIED TREASURE
by Michele Jakubowski

The Sleuths of Somerville
THE PROFESSOR'S DISCOVERY
by Michele Jakubowski

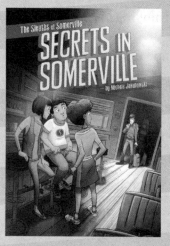

The Sleuths of Somerville
SECRETS IN SOMERVILLE
by Michele Jakubowski

The Sleuths of Somerville
TOUR OF TROUBLE
by Michele Jakubowski